The World's
Your Lobster

BLOOMSBURY CHILDREN'S
POETRY TITLES

ISBN 0 7475 3866 2

ISBN 0 7475 3864 6

ISBN 0 7475 3865 4

ISBN 0 7475 3863 8

The World's Your Lobster

THE VERY BEST
COLLECTED POEMS BY
ADRIAN HENRI

Illustrated by
Wendy Smith

BLOOMSBURY
CHILDREN'S
BOOKS

First published in Great Britain in 1998
Bloomsbury Publishing Plc, 38 Soho Square, London, W1V 5DF

Copyright © Text Adrian Henri 1998
Copyright © Illustrations Wendy Smith 1998

The moral right of the author has been asserted
A CIP catalogue record of this book is available from the
British Library

ISBN 0 7475 3864 6

Printed in England by Clays Ltd, St Ives plc

10 9 8 7 6 5 4 3 2 1

Contents

Poets

can't compete
with clowns.
When they try to juggle words
they trip over nouns,
drop their 'h's
trap their verbs between the pages,
try to pull rhymes out of a hat,
adjectives that just fall flat;
sentences that fail to start,
paragraphs that come apart.

Clowns can tumble,
clowns can fumble,
clowns can laugh
and clowns can grumble.

Everybody
loves a clown:
no one laughs
when the poet falls down.

Domestic Help

The other day,
one of our domestic robots went mad,
kissed my dad,
poured marmalade over the videowall,
shampooed the cat,
sugared my mother's hair,
and sat on my sister's knee
(she fell through the chair).

Dad's frantic fiddling with the control-panel
only made matters worse.

It vacuum-cleaned the ceiling,
put the coffee-table into the garbage disposal
    unit,
uncorked a bottle of wine
and poured it gently over the carpet,
then carefully unscrewed its head
and deposited it in Mum's lap.

Mother says
that's the way it is these days:
you can't get the robots you used to.

Best Friends

It's Susan I talk to not Tracey,
Before that I sat next to Jane;
I used to be best friends with Lynda
But these days I think she's a pain.

Natasha's all right in small doses,
I meet Mandy sometimes in town;
I'm jealous of Annabel's pony
And I don't like Nicola's frown.

I used to go skating with Catherine,
Before that I went there with Ruth;
And Kate's so much better at trampoline:
She's a showoff, to tell you the truth.

I think that I'm going off Susan,
She borrowed my comb yesterday;
I *think* I might sit next to Tracey,
She's my nearly best friend: she's OK.

Not Me!

Every little girl would like to be
the fairy on the Christmas tree
except me.
I'd rather be
a Kung-Fu fighter like Bruce Lee.

Every little girl would like to be
The Queen of the May
and reign for a day.
I'd rather stow away
and hitch-hike across the USA.

Every little girl would like to be
a bridesmaid or a bride;
not me. I'd rather ride
a motorbike. Or hide
inside a pirate's cave. Or save
a penalty-kick at Wembley.
Or have the Secret Service send me
on missions as a spy. Or fly
a shuttle into space. Or race
against Sebastian Coe. I know
what other little girls would like to be

Not me!

Fashion

Me?
I wouldn't be seen
dead in one . . .
I know Sharon's got one
and Kevin's sister
what's-her-name;
all the same,
anything that Jayne wears
can't be any good . . .

I suppose I *could*
just try it and see . . .
Well, why not?
Everyone else has got
one,
why not me?

Sammy the Flying Piglet

See him fly!
See him fly!
See the piglet in the sky!

Off to Athens
Off to Rome
Over France then straight back home
for tea:
thought Sammy 'This is the life
for me'

Even before
he ever flew
little Sammy always knew
he only had to try
and one day
he'd fly.

'What?
Pigs fly?
When Nelson gets his eye
back' his mother would grunt
'One day' thought Sammy,
the runt of the litter,
'I'll show them'

See him fly!
See him fly!
A piglet hurtling
across the sky –
Eight miles high!

Over valleys, over hills,
dodging pylons, dodging mills,
chasing cattle, scaring sheep,
loop the loop
then straight back home
to sleep.

All the others on the farm
viewed his skills with some alarm
'Heavens! What's he doing now?
Bless us all!' said the oldest cow
'A flying pig? Whatever next?'
Even his brothers felt quite vexed
standing earthbound by their trough
while the smallest pig took off.

See him fly!
See him fly!
That's our Sammy
in the sky!
Heaven knows why!

Off to Athens
Off to Rome
Over Spain and then again
back home:
thought Sammy 'This is the life
for me

I'm free!

Whoopee!'

Adios Amigos . . .

¡THE MEXICANS ARE COMING!
The whisper goes round the school
persistent as the smell of garlic.
Strange sounds come from the kitchens,
Mariachi Bands and maraccas,
Shouts of 'Olé'. They're going crackers.

¡THE MEXICANS ARE HERE!
Rumour spreads, hot as chilli-powder.
The dinner-ladies burst through the kitchen
  door
clapping their hands, stamping their heels on
  the floor.
Brightly-coloured shawls swirl. Boys and girls
watch, wide-eyed as a bullfight crowd.

¡THE MEXICANS HAVE COME!
Michelle's mum serves Tropical Dessert
with a flick of her skirt. Her friends serve
Chile con Chips, Baked Beans y Tortillas
wearing black lace mantillas. It tastes
really nice, and it's just the same price.

¡THE MEXICANS HAVE BEEN!
They haven't been seen for days. Just aprons
   of green
and the clatter of trays. Distant as holidays
and a tropical moon. I hope they come back
   soon.
The Headmaster's put his sombrero away.
'Cos nothing's the same since that wonderful
   day
when we all cried 'Olé',
     when the Mexicans came . . .

Rhinestone Rhino

Ah'm a rhinestone rhino
From the lone star state
Ah'm a Country 'n' Western
All time great

Ah'm a ten-ton Texas
Bunch o'joy
Ah'm a rhin-o-ceros
Good ol' boy

Ah'm a rhinestone rhino –
ceros yodel-ay-ee

At the Grand Old Opry
Ah'm a superstar
When ah sings ma songs
And strums ma guit-ar

Ah began ma life
In a country shack
Now ah rides around
In a Cad-ill-ac

Ah'm a rhinestone rhino –
ceros yodel-ay-ee

There's Tammy 'n' Dolly 'n'
Emmy Lou
And Johnny Cash is King
It's true

But the pride of Gnashville,
Tennessee
Is your five-by-five star
Lil' ol' me

Ah'm a rhinestone Rhino –
ceros yodel-ay-ee

Ah'm a rhine –
    stone
      rhino

    ceros
    yodel
      ay –
        eeee

Pedestrian

I've got a pain in the 96th,
or is it the 97th? I can never
remember. That side's left,
this is . . . yes, that's right,
the 96th. It's all the spiky bits
on this green thing. Oh!
now the 47th's started
to go . . . soon
I won't have one left
to stand on.

Square Meal

He kept a pet hyena
And then he bought a flock
He fed them all on Oxo cubes
And made a laughing stock.

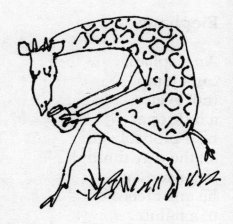

Paracetamol

for Spike Sterne

If a giraffe has a headache
Or a chimpanzee has a fall
There's no aspirins in the jungle
'Cause the parrots ate 'em all.

Elephants

An elephant
can't jump
(not even
a little one)
he'd probably go
all the way through
to Australia;
he must feel a bit
of a failure.

On the other hand,
a whale can jump
right out of the water.
A camel can lift his hump
above the desert sands.
Emus and yaks
leap in the air
without a care.
Even a hippopotamus
won't sink to the bottomless
depths of the river,
even though his weight
makes the ground quiver
when he lands.
As for the chimpanzee
he can land on his hands
if he wants to.

But what can the poor elephant do?

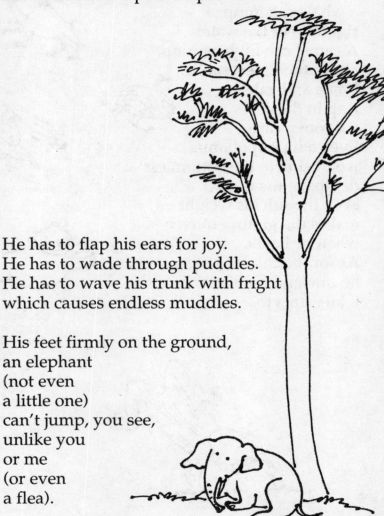

He has to flap his ears for joy.
He has to wade through puddles.
He has to wave his trunk with fright
which causes endless muddles.

His feet firmly on the ground,
an elephant
(not even
a little one)
can't jump, you see,
unlike you
or me
(or even
a flea).

City Hedges

There are pinstripe hedges
Trees wear bowler hats
Bushes like umbrellas
All the cows wear spats

Fish commute downriver
Rush to catch the tide
Birds clock in at daybreak
Lunchbox by their side

The banks are full of blackberries
With walls of thistledown
The sheep are in the typing-pool:

The country's come to town!

In a Field

Here's two more of them:
the funny ones with only two legs,
no horns,
and hardly any hair.

Yes, little ones this time
I'll go and have a closer look.

I know,
Let's follow them. For fun.

Look!
They've started to run . . .

Rover

for David Ross

I have a pet oyster called Rover.
He lives in the bathroom sink
and is never any trouble:
no birdseed or tins of Kennomeat,
no cat-litter.
We don't need to take him for walks,
we don't need an oyster-flap in the back door.

He doesn't bark
or sing,
just lies in the sink
and never says a thing.
Sometimes,
when he feels irritable,
he grits his teeth
and produces a little pearl.

At night,
we tuck him up snug in his oyster-bed
until the bathroom tide comes in
in the morning.

Sometimes
I look at Rover and say
'The world's your lobster,
Rover', I say.

A Poem for my Cat

You're black and sleek and beautiful
What a pity your best friends won't tell you
Your breath smells of Kit-E-Kat.

Conversation on a Garden Wall

Move over, you've got all the bricks with the
   sun on.

Oh, all right. Mind you, I was here first.

He came round after me again last night.
Right up to the back door.

Really? He's persistent, I'll say that for him.

I'll say. Anyway, they chased him away.

How are yours treating you?

Not too bad, really.
They're a bit careful with the milk.

Oh, mine are all right about that. They're a bit
unimaginative with my food, though. Last week
I had the same meal every day.

You don't say. The food's OK. It's a real pain
being pushed out in the rain. Every night, rain or
snow, out I go.

Me, too. Look, here he is back again.

Cheek. Pretend to take no notice.

At least you've got a quiet place with none of
those small ones around. I hardly get a minute.

That's true. All mine do is sit in front of
a little box with tiny ones inside it.

Mine do too. It's the only peace I get.

And one of them pushes that noisy thing
round the floor every day.

Terrible, isn't it? Mind you,
mine only does it once or twice a week.

You're lucky. Oh, the sun's gone in.

Yes, time for a stroll. I'll jump down and
just sort of walk past him, accidentally.

Accidentally on purpose, you mean.
See you round.

Yes, see you around. I'll tell you one thing,
though.

What's that?

It's a good job they can't talk,
isn't it?

H25

Hedgehogs hog the hedges,
  roadhogs hog the roads:
I'd like to build a motorway
  for badgers, frogs and toads,
with halts for hungry hedgehogs
  at an all-night service station;
four lanes wide and free from man
  right across the nation.
Free from oil and petrol fumes,
  and free from motor cars,
to see the busy hedghogs trot
  underneath the stars.

Queen Tut

Fancy
a mummy
all shut up
in a great big case
with a nasty face;
when you see them
in a museum
it's fine:
but I'm glad she's
Tutankhamun
's mum,
not mine.

Forecast

The East Wind doth blow,
and we shall have snow,
and what will Cock Robin do then,
poor thing?

He'll turn up the heating,
store tinned worms for eating,
and not leave his bed until Spring,
wise thing.

Short Poem

I'm the shortest
in our year.
If you wrote a poem
about me
it'd only reach
to here . . .

The Further Adventures of Sammy the Flying Piglet

Sammy the Piglet went to France
to teach the ladies how to dance
flew from the farm to the Eiffel Tower
(with a following wind) in half an hour.

He went to Oxford to learn to spell,
flew round a quad and was scared by the bell;
he played with the students and lectured the
    dons,
took off from a punt and frightened the
    swans.

Now sometimes when he's really bored
he leaves the farm to race Concorde;
then back over London to look at the Queen:
his mother never knows where he's been.

Since little Sammy learned to fly
he's hardly ever in the sty;
up, up and away, high in the air
he swoops and dives without a care.

Up, up above the world so high,
a flying pig in the clear blue sky.

The Dark

I don't like the dark coming down on my head
It feels like a blanket thrown over the bed
I don't like the dark coming down on my head

I don't like the dark coming down over me
It feels like the room's full of things I can't see
I don't like the dark coming down over me

There isn't enough light from under the door
It only just reaches the edge of the floor
There isn't enough light from under the door

I wish that my dad hadn't put out the light
It feels like there's something that's just out of
   sight
I wish that my dad hadn't put out the light

But under the bedclothes it's warm and secure
You can't see the ceiling you can't see the floor
Yes, under the bedclothes it's warm and secure
So I think I'll stay here till it's daylight once more.

The Haunted Disco

When it's half-past three in the morning
right through to break of day,
a phantom DJ opens up
for the dead to come and play.

The coloured lights are flashing,
and the crowd are on their feet,
but there's no sound of them dancing
to the ghostly disco-beat.

When there's ice between your shoulders,
and the hairs rise on your neck,
and you don't know who you're dancing with
at the haunted discotheque.

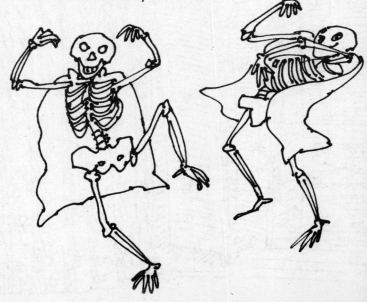

When you daren't look at your partner,
and you fear their bony hand,
the go-go ghosts all boogie
to an ancient, nameless band.

The graveyard sounds are all around
the mist drifts everywhere,
but the ghastly crowds in mini-shrouds
rave on without a care.

When there's ice between your shoulders,
and the hairs rise on your neck,
and you know you'll dance for ever
in the haunted discotheque.

I Saw

I'm *sure*
I saw a dinosaur
just across the road,
peeping out above Tesco
and the DIY store.
I did,
just before:
there's an enormous foot-mark
on the car park
and a Ford Escort
squashed flat; apart from that
there's an awful mess
where it looks like something's tripped
over a skip.

There was
that awful sound, too,
just like thunder, or the noise
the bin-lorries make
when they chew up the rubbish.

Perhaps I should go and investigate.

On second thoughts,
I think I'll just wait.

The Lurkers

On our Estate
When it's getting late
In the middle of the night
They come in flocks
From beneath tower-blocks
And crawl towards the light

Down the Crescent
Up the Drive
Late at night
They come alive
Lurking here and lurking there
Sniffing at the midnight air

Up the Shopping Centre
You might just hear their call
Something like a bin-bag
Moving by the wall

Lurking at the bus-stop
Seen through broken glass
Something dark and slimy
Down the underpass

On our Estate
When it's getting late
In the middle of the night
There are things that lurk
About their work
Till dawn puts them to flight.

Nightmare Cemetery

Don't go down with me today
to Nightmare Cemetery
You don't know what you'll see today
in Nightmare Cemetery

Don't go through the gates today
to Nightmare Cemetery
You don't know what waits today
in Nightmare Cemetery

Don't go down the lane today
to Nightmare Cemetery
There you might remain today
in Nightmare Cemetery

Don't go down the road today
to Nightmare Cemetery
Haunt of bat and toad today
in Nightmare Cemetery

The sun will never shine today
in Nightmare Cemetery
Horrors wait in line today
in Nightmare Cemetery

Close the gates and step inside
Much too late to try and hide
Hear the hinges creak with glee
I'll be waiting, just you see,
You're here for ever, just like me
in Nightmare Cemetery.

Autumn Haiku

the high-pitched laughter
of girls outside swirls like leaves
on the Autumn wind.

Haiku: City Park in Winter

snowdrops stand up stiff
twilight nurses
round the darkening flowerbeds.

48

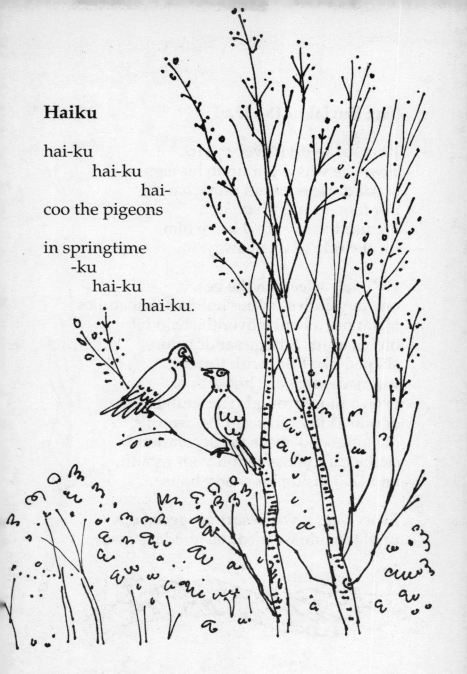

Haiku

hai-ku
    hai-ku
        hai-
coo the pigeons

in springtime
   -ku
     hai-ku
       hai-ku.

The Burial of the Dad

We used to do it every year.
There he was, right up to his ears
in sand. He couldn't move hand
nor foot, let alone stand.
We used to say we'd leave him
for the tide to wash away.

He'd fall asleep on the beach,
one day each summer holiday. Sometimes
Mum put a hanky over the bald bit
on his head. A huge sandcastle
shaped like Dad, with turrets
we made with our buckets, or
even a moat around. The sound
of other kids and seagulls, armfuls
of stones and shells for decoration,
sticky candyfloss round your mouth,
and Dad inside his sandy house.

Every year it was a sort of special day
until the tide washed the holidays away.

Rosie the Rhino

Rosie the Rhino lives on my bed
but dreams of a pool by a swamp instead;
Rosie the Rhino dreams at night
of a clearing where the sun is bright:
all I can hear is cars in the street,
but she hears the suck of squelching feet.
Rosie the Rhino is soft and grey,
she dreams by night and sleeps by day:
safe by my pillow she will never know
the pain of the hunter's savage blow,
the helpless horn that's torn from the head
while she dreams on in a city bed.

Song of the Earth

Look deep into the hidden world of ponds.
Mosses, tadpoles, the gently-moving fronds
of water-crowfoot. Help clean up
this tiny world. Curled tendrils of fern
peer hopefully through bin-bags, chip-papers,
choke on polystyrene. Green water
fights for its breath amid the stink of sewage,
black rainbows of oil. Mersey and Alt,
Dee and Weaver leave a cry for help
with every tide. Our leavings mark
their riverside.

So bring in your wellies, bring in your macs,
never mind sore feet or aching backs.

Take a dawn walk on Hilbre. Wait
in the silvery light to see the birds migrate.
Clean up the Lowfields, clean up the beach,
clear the canal and footpath, each of you
can find one small thing to do
to reciprocate. Give back the gifts
of scabious and celandine, wood anemone
and wild garlic, before it's too late.

So bring binoculars, notebook and pen,
this land can be green and pleasant again.

Families lark in the mud to trace the tiny
   creatures.
A pond made safe for toads. Behind the
   motorways,
the access-roads, the land shyly reveals its
   features.
In Kirkby a wood grows where one nearly died;
look inside: see how new life starts
beneath tyres and tin cans, boxes and shopping-
   carts.

So bring your raincoats, bring your boots,
dig in the earth and find your roots.

Life is short but the earth is long
put your ear to the ground and hear its song.

Dusty Bluebells

This is the night
when all the trees hide their heads
and wait for the shooting stars to fall
their tails tangled in the poplars

In and out the dusty bluebells
In and out the dusty bluebells
In and out the dusty bluebells
I will be your lover

This is the night
when light dimples the water
in a world so still
it takes nine years to hear the leaves move

Pitter-patter pitter-patter on my shoulder
Pitter-patter pitter-patter on my shoulder
Pitter-patter pitter-patter on my shoulder
You will be my lover

This is the night
when cattle stand like statues
when waterfalls hold their breath
and listen for the nightingale

In and out the dusty bluebells
In and out the dusty bluebells
In and out the dusty bluebells
I will be your lover

This is the night
when all the dandelion-clocks blow at once
and it is midnight
for ever.

Kate

I think I'm in love with Kate
it can't just be her dimples
it's not as simple
as that.

Shirley's blonde and Sue's hair's red
and curly. But I like dark hair
short and straight
like Kate.

I think that I'm too late.
She'll go straight home. Perhaps
she'll wait and say
'Hello'.

I'll walk home past her street.
Perhaps I'll meet her on the way.
I won't know what
to say.

I pulled her hair and called her names today.
She ran away. I'm *sure* she knows
that I'm in love
with Kate.

I ♡ Kate

Skipping Song

A word in time
saves nine
Skip a word
and save a rhyme
Save a word
and skip a rhyme
A word in time
saves nine

A word in time
saves nine
Skip a line
and miss a rhyme
Miss a line
and skip a rhyme
A word in time
saves nine

The last line's coming
the last line's coming
the last line's coming

Ready or not.

Autumn

Season of conkers and fireworks
and mellow fruitfulness. New shoes,
and a coat that's a bit too big,
to grow into next year. Blackberries
along the canal, white jungles
of frost on the window. Leaves
to kick all the way home,
the smell of bonfires,
stamping the ice on puddles
into crazy paving. The nights come in
early, and you can't play out
after school. Soon
there'll be tangerines in the shops,
in shiny paper like Christmas lights.

The little ones write letters to Santa Claus.

The big ones laugh under the streetlights.

Lullaby

Imagine being asleep in the deep
Counting whales instead of sheep.

Morning Break

Eleven O'Clock:
seagulls noisy as children
pick up crisps from the empty playground.

Early Spring

Daffodils shiver,
huddle away from the wind,
like people waiting at a bus-stop.

The Phantom Lollipop Lady

The phantom lollipop lady
haunts the crossroads
where the old school used to be;
they closed it down in 1973.

The old lollipop lady
loved her job, and stood there
for seven years altogether,
no matter how bad the weather.

When they pulled the old school down
she still stood there every day:
a pocketful of sweets for the little ones,
smiles and a joke for the big ones.

One day the lollipop lady
was taken away to hospital.
Without her standing there
the corner looked, somehow, bare.

After a month and two operations
the lollipop lady died;
the children felt something missing:
she had made her final crossing.
Now if you go down alone at dusk

just before the streetlights go on,
look closely at the corner over there:
in the shadows by the lamp-post you'll see
 her.

Helping phantom children across the street,
holding up the traffic with a ghostly hand;
at the twilight crossing where four roads meet
the phantom lollipop lady stands.

The Heart Poem

the hands of the clock move
minute
by minute   by minute   by minute

the digits shift
second
by second   by second   by second

arteries slow
minute
by minute   by minute   by minute

veins stiffen
second
by second   by second   by second

the last tube-train
pulls into the platform
minute
by minute   by minute   by minute